Stor es

To d

GREATHOUSE HORRORS

Author's Note & Content Warning

It is hard for anyone to guess on what kind of content will be received as damaging to another, so please be advised, this story is a brutal one – most of my work is.

My intention is not to shock and scar my readers, but to reflect that life itself can often become just as menacing in the blink of an eye. It is a dash of realism that I find enjoyable in the works of horror I consume as a reader and so some dark tropes have woven their way into my fictional Nightmares as well.

It is true that my inspiration for these twisted tales comes from my insecurities, fears, and painful hardships. Just keep in mind that these characters are fictional entities and not how I perceive myself or anyone from my personal life.

I have listed above some of the more alarming plot points, if any of those seem off-putting, please do not continue this story.

Enjoy my nightmares

Locked Away

Where Memories Are Made

The Perfect Life

Locked

Away

*D*riving so long will make your ass feel like it has fallen off. It did not help that traffic was horrible, bumper to bumper kind of horrible, but we made it to the cabin safe and sound. And yes, both our asses are still intact. I parked the car and quickly turned the key. I was desperately anticipating the sound from the engine to gently fade into the silence that consumed the wooded area around us. *I am more than ready to hear the nothingness.*

I had waited so long for this opportunity to breathe in the crisp fall air. It remained untouched by the fumes of busy city life that we had just fled from. I looked around; the view was, well, beautifully breathtaking. Such a simple way to describe something so majestic, I know, but this is a simple place of escape. A place where the mind was free to wander.

We sat there, blanketed by our own internal thoughts as we took in the scenery. There was one single break in the tree line, and it surrounded the cabin and the crescent moon shaped lake behind it perfectly. Almost as if the trees were guarding this place from anyone who dared to mistreat what it was meant to be.

The treetops made waves of color in the soft breeze, and I could hear the faint sound from the rustling leaves that were dancing in the wind. It appears nature itself was playing a welcome home melody that soothed the soul. This was my happy place. The place where I became the best version of myself.

And just like that, I was being pulled down the rabbit hole of my memories, recalling why the presence felt here was so magical. This quiet little county nook had both broke and rebuilt me all at once. I had learned to love myself for all that I am. All my flaws, mistakes, regrets… I had accepted each of them, right there on that dock.

My eyes drifted away from the distant lake and my mind returned to what was happening now. Still, I continued to sit my car, basking in the comforting silence my friend and I was sharing. I gave her a brief glance, just long enough to try and read her face. *Was she happy?*
I suppose it does not matter, not in this moment. Afterall, happiness is subjective and if she *were* happy then this trip would not be happening. *She will find happiness here;* I assured myself before allowing my mind to drift back to my past journey through self-awakening.

It all happened over a decade ago. Yet now, in this moment, the memory seemed much more recent. The night was quiet, much like it is right now. My long dark hair danced in the wind, stirring up the water from the lake and causing it to mist my skin, leaving it to glisten in the moonlight like the bright stars that filled the night's sky. Despite the wind however, the water was still able to mimic a mirror quite well.

I stared into my reflection, my eyes looking back with a fierce determination to thrive. It was funny, in a way, that I had initially came to this place with the intention of never leaving it again. I was ready to be born back into the stars above, to find eternal peace, but instead of finding death, I found life.

I continued to examine the face. It felt like I was seeing it for the first time. The slender pink lips never abandoned a slightly haunting smile. It appears my own reflection was studying me as well, silently judging as they viewed what was locked away deep inside my mind.

At that exact moment, I realized how beautiful I truly am. Suddenly I was overwhelmed with a new thought, the thought of growing old. My heart began to race at the thought of losing the beauty I could finally see. 18 years wasted on a blind illusion. An illusion that I was just able to shatter. My breathing seemed to be in a race with my heart, and in that moment of pure inner chaos a calm swept over me, as I accepted who I really was and what I had to do.

"Well, here we are!" I exclaimed to my friend, snapping out of my reverie. "This is going to be the best retreat yet!"

I could not hold in my excitement any longer. I was like a teenage girl about to have my first sleepover. *And I gave her more than enough time to feel through her emotions.*

I reached for the handle as if I were reaching for my desires and the wind welcomed my arrival, catching the door in its path and forcing it open. Instantly my heart filled with certainty in my decision. It was time to go.

With animated motions matching how childlike and bubbly I felt, I glided my way around the car. The sound of the gravel scattering beneath my flower-print sneakers cut through the air and instantly drew attention to just how eerie this place was. *There is always a threat lurking beneath the surface of any beautiful thing, and a place of beauty is no different.*

It was so calm here. Too calm. I knew Ruth would be sensing that by now and it was obvious that my upbeat personality was failing. There was not a bird in sight, no squirrels playing through the branches or even an insect buzzing through the air. There was only the wind.

I pressed my way closer to the passenger side of the car, confused at why Ruth remained inside. Gently I leaned against the window, gazing into the tear-filled eyes of my soul-searching bestie. She looked so tense and worried. *This retreat will rid her of that forever.*

"Relax and look around, connect with your other senses. If it helps you calm down, I could tell you a story?" I continue to stare down at her, waiting for a response. Slowly she nodded. *Poor girl.*

I let out a sigh and stared off into the woods, thinking of the only story fitting enough to tell. The same story that drew Ruth to me as a guide through her own journey. Sure, she knew most of what I was about to say. But there were hidden facts that I had kept back intentionally, all so I could elaborate on them here, in this setting.

I had met Ruth through a support group for beginner witches. It was a small-town coffee shop group that formed together through a bulletin board flyer made from recycled paper. It was the sheer cuteness and desperation that captured my attention, but it was Ruth who made me stay through that first meeting of utter nonsense and an alarming amount of cultural appropriation.

That small group was so far from anything of value, let alone magic. Yet Ruth seemed to bear a sliver of hope. We had only been chatting for three weeks after meetings, but despite that, I was finally able to convince her to come out to my safe space to do some soul searching of her own.

She was so dedicated to the group that planning anything outside of what she considered her coven made her uneasy to say the least. *Yet here we are.* I looked back down at her, giving her a reassuring smile.

"Imagine you are the most powerful person in history. We are talking past, present, and future. You have the ability to end world hunger with a wave of your hand, but also the power to destroy an entire country with a single thought." I elaborately used my hands to help express the severity of what I was telling her.

"Sounds like you'd be a pretty dangerous person, huh?" My mood began to change slightly. I was less enthusiastic as I reached a detail that still pained my soul at the very core. "Well, my great-great-aunt Grace thought so. You see, I do not have to imagine what it would be like to possess that much power. I just have to imagine what my Grace had foreseen that caused her to lock my power away before ever giving me a chance to choose a different path." I could hear how bitter I sounded. Ashamed that I might be coming off as if I were drowning in self-pity, I focused in on Ruth to read her expression. *Ah yes, more confusion stirring in those eyes.*

"Yes, Ruth. I am speaking about real power. Real witches. None of this manifesting greatness bullshit the coven has been feeding you, but real unworldly abilities.

"And no, not everyone has the gift. But you... You have a little secret swimming in your blood, which is why we are here. Why I am telling you all of this.

"You see, no other witch in history has ever had their power locked away before their birth. Regardless of how horrendous their path could be, they were allowed the freedom to choose. Now you're probably thinking, *well, you could destroy the world!* That is most definitely true, and exactly why I pointed it out, but evidently there is a far worse fate that one could bestow the world."

I slumped myself forward, still pushing most of my weight against the car, but dropping my attention from Ruth. "I get it. This is a lot to take in at one time, but you must understand that this one-sided conversation... it is beneficial to me, truly.

"The thing is Ruth, there are so many different types of witches in the world, and each has power that helps contain balance. Some see the ever-changing future, some speak to the dead, while others can perform what can only be defined as miracles. Obviously, Grace was a Visioned Witch, and you might have guessed that they tend to be rather powerful. They would have to be, right? To be able to lock away someone's gift.

"What could make her do that? What would be worse than destroying the world? I really wish those were questions I could answer, but it seems protecting the world from me was her dying wish." I couldn't stop myself, like an uncontrollable hiccup, a crazed giggle escaped my lips as I continued, "The fuckery of this is if you knew how many times the world has already been destroyed then you would see this more from my perspective. Every single end of the world prediction has come true and then some!

"The Earth itself is magical. Some argue that it is the one who blesses mankind with the gifts we have, but the only thing we are sure of is that every time we destroy it, it rebuilds itself as it was or wants to be.

"There is no way I can explain how or why it does this, no one can, but I can tell you the Earth has a soft spot for humans and their inventions. However, at the end of the day it will put its own wellbeing first. Always.

"There have been many times the higher witches have had to step in an assist in the rebuilding. Which is also why magic is everywhere, hiding in plain sight.

"It is a part of science, religion and especially, in politics. We have all heard the conspiracy theories, about a group trying to obtain New World Order...

"Well, that group does exist, but it is way more boring than it sounds and nothing like what people think.

"It's all in the name really. They are nothing more than guardians and only called upon when needed, whether that be when the countries of the world turn on one another over greed or when an evil person makes the wrong choice.

"Of course, even though the Earth does do most of the heavy lifting, the group is still necessary. They are also generally the individuals who pass punishment if another witch abuses their gift and disrupts the balance. These punishments can consist of memory cleansing, death, or worse, to have their powers locked away.

"It all depends on the crime, but destroying the world is typically the fastest way to have your powers yanked. So, you can see my conflict.

"I had broken 0 laws, yet here I am, a middle-aged woman who has lived one confusing life." I gently opened the door for Ruth. She was being extremely jumpy for someone who was currently surrounded by nature.

"I'm sure you're ready to stretch your legs a bit. How about we walk down to the dock, and if you want, I can finish my story there." I pointed ahead of us to the few bits of sparkling water you could see between the tall blades of overgrown grass.

She seemed apprehensive at first but agreed, nodding. We walked in silence down the gravel path with our arms interlocked. Neither of us seemed to be in much of a hurry. Instead, we both looked around, taking everything in.

The grass was a perfect shade of green that complemented the multi-shades of red and yellows that were scattered across the treetops. It all just looked like a painting. It did not seem like something this breathtaking could be real, regardless of how many times I had been here. Each time felt brand new.

Slowly we reached our way to the end of the dock that stretched out from the curve of the lake. Ruth sat down with her legs crossed. *She really seems so uptight. It is kind of kill-*

ing the mood, really. I could feel my facial expression begin to match my annoyed inner thoughts.

"You want to hear more?" I asked in a rushed tone.

I need to be more patient with her, this is probably so overwhelming.

There might still be a breeze blowing through the trees, yet there is no other sound from nature, just stillness. To a stressed and anxious mind, quiet can be a defining sound. Ruth looked over at me, eyes trembling, and she slowly nodded her head, yes. I gave her a comforting smile and patted her leg softly as I sat down beside her.

"I was about three years old when I realized there was something locked deep inside my mind. I was unaware of what it was... What I was. There was no hint that I had powers and no guidance to warn me of what would come to those who attempted to unlock what was taken.

"Once a witch has their powers locked away there is no chance of getting them back. And death would undoubtedly follow those who tried. Unknowing of why or what I was doing, I tried.

"I dug deep into my subconscious, and almost paid the price, but I unlocked a tiny sliver of my power. For three -year-old me, that was enough. Of course, my mom immediately rushed me to the doctor thinking that her only child was moments away from dying from some medical issue. It did not help that on paper the doctors called what I had done to my brain "meningitis." Really, they had no idea what was wrong with me, but by the time I arrived to get checked out, I had mostly recovered.

"As I got older though, I grew to be more of a normal person, my unlocked abilities were nothing more than party tricks that any Touched One could muster." With that information Ruth's eyes seemed more confused than ever, but she was never one to ask questions, it wasn't very polite, or whatever her mom raised her to believe. So, I leaned in as I explained, "A Touched One is a person who has been touched by magic, in some way. Magic is so strong that it can leave a residue on anything or anyone it contacts, infecting them like a disease for bloodlines to come." She seemed to be understanding a little more, at least easing up a bit. Ruth's gaze was now fixated more on the cabin, but she still sat there in the car with her hands pressed tightly in her lap as she made quick glances towards the long dirt road we had come. I sighed, wishing that she'd be a little more openminded while I reminded myself that she was at least listening to what I was saying.

Eagerly I continued, "My party tricks were a variation of low-level mind reading, manipulating elements, soothing animals with just a touch, etcetera. Sure, they sound impressive, but I promise they are not. And they are also easily faked. But a Touched One is what you are, Ruth, and I am so sorry you have not got to experience that part of yourself fully.

"Knowing what I know now I often wonder if it was a blessing that I was assumed to be nothing more than a Touched One. See, it took me a long time to figure out what that even was, let alone recalling a full memory from my toddler days of what I had done. What I accomplished.

"So right before my tenth birthday, my great-great-grandmother, GG as I called her, requested that I spend the weekend with her. No doubt that I was less than thrilled to go, but also no surprise that I ended up enjoying GG's company.

"She spilled the beans on everything. Which is how I found out. Thanks GG!" I shouted to the lake. "Despite knowing the truth, I was sixteen by the time I really started to believe. One day is what caused my memories to completely resurface and GG's words to stand out.

"I was spending my summer working at this hole-in-the-wall diner. You know the type, almost like the coffee shop you and I met at. But this was a little more rustic and the regulars were either elderly folk hanging desperately to their daily routines as if that will prolong their life, or the random group of teens who would try and rebrand the corner booths as the hottest place to be.

"Even this place had the one strange regular who everyone either tried to avoid or go out of their way to greet… I typically tried to avoid everyone at this point in my teenage angsty years, still this odd woman approached me, wanting to read my aura.

"She was such a sweet witch, and I was still considered the newbie there, so she had never really had a chance to read my aura, which was her gift and one she could freely use in the open without question.

"Eager to wow me with what she could see, she rushed over and grabbed my hand with such excitement. Gently she rubbed her thumbs on the palm of my hand, and then this look of horror washed over her face. She dropped my hand like I had burned her with my touch, grabbed her purse from the counter, and left.

"She never did come back during my shifts. The stares from my co-workers and patrons sent chills down my spine. They were looking at me like I was monster. It was remarkably like the look that you've been giving me this whole time."

Ruth's eyes widened. She quickly started to sway her body back and forth, trying to inch herself away from me, but remaining cautious of the narrow dock. Tears started streaming down her cheeks and I can only imagine that the muffled noise she was making were pleas for me to let her go. *So sweet.*

"Ruth, honestly, you're ruining story time. This trip was all about searching for yourself, remember? How can you expect to find yourself and face your demons, if you can't even bear to look at me without fear?" I was hoping my mini speech would pull her back into a semi-calm stage, but these tears of hers were like waterfalls.

I learned back and laid down on the dock so that I could look up at the clouds. I closed my eyes for just a few moments to regain my own inner peace, and then I heard the splash.

"Are. You. Serious?" I growled. Red water splashed across the dock, my clothes, my face and Ruth was in the lake. This was not going how I pictured it would go at all.

I more envisioned that Ruth would have sat still, like a good little sacrifice, and waited patiently before I got to do my favorite part. I mean, it wasn't like she was the first person I had pulled one over on. Oh no, I was a professional at this point. The steps were simple: Befriend, drug, tie up and kidnap, then pretend to cut them free before delivering the blade deep into their throat...

Free will and human impulse will always surprise you. I watched for a few moments as Ruth thrashed around in the water, unable to easily move with her arms tied up from her wrists to her elbows and her ankles wrapped with weights. *She really did not think this through.*

"I wanted to finish my story first, Ruth," I huffed as I stood up. "However, this trip is about you after all, so if you prefer to get this over with now, then who am I to deny your last request." I hopped down to the bank, just shy of where Ruth's head bobbed on the surface. Bubbles rose around her until they slowly stopped.

I kept close to the bank, not wanting to risk myself sliding into to the water. I was not sure how deep the crescent moon lake was, but I knew there was not a favorable descend into the depths, just a plummet. I stretched my arm out grabbing onto those beautiful locks of hair that were floating on top of the water and pulled Ruth towards me.

The moment her mouth resurfaced she naturally began to cough and gag. *Seems the tape across her face was not as waterproof as the label suggested.*

"Shhhhh," I soothed, caressing her cheek with my fingertips.

"What do you want from me?" Ruth pushed out.

"I want you to let your fear bleed out into this lake. It's time to let it go." With my other hand I pulled out my pocketknife and flung the blade open. "Let it all go, Ruth. Let go of your stress, your worry, your pain, and give it to the lake." I smiled, pressing the knife against her chin and in one swift motion I slit her throat. This was not my first victim, but for this purpose, she was finally my last. I pushed her bleeding corpse a little further out, hoping she would be free from the embankment as well as life itself.

I guess the rest of my story does not have to be told out loud. After that day in the diner, my curiosity of why that woman reacted to me the way she did, consumed my every thought.

I took an interest in spirit boards and surrounded myself with other so-called witches. Of course, there were not any real witches that joined my group. Bloodlines do not tend to mingle with Touched Ones and despite me know the full truth of my power, I did not feel it safe to advertise that I was not Touched...

Through the spirit board most of my questions were answered, or more so that I was pointed in the direction my answers resided. Sacrifice.

For over ten years I worked to fund the building of this cabin, using this place as my own personal alter. The lake itself was a hidden treasure that I was not willing to give up. Its origin was unknown to the rest of the world, at least

Locked Away

to the world of normal.

To the witches, however, this lake is said to be the last gift bestowed to all covens to share, as a place to wash the negative powers away. But as the years passed, so did the need for witches to seek out this place.

And with so many polluting it with the hope that it would absorb anything malicious, those who did remember this place stayed clear of it, too afraid that its purifying abilities had been lost.

But for me, I was counting on all those hardships to still be swimming beneath the surface. Using the blood of the sacrificed along with the positive energy the lake still clung to, and the energy it had consumed from witches long ago, I was attempting to create a powerful surge of magic. One that would restore me by drinking the energy that surges through the now tainted water.

I walked back to the dock and stopped at the end. Ruth's body was already being pulled into the depths by the weights. Eagerly I leaned over the water and cupped my hands. *This is it. This is what I had worked so hard for.* I put my hands in the crimson water and drank my fill, focusing my mind on the incantation needed. There was no delay. Immediately the power was intense. My mind felt like it was melting, my veins burned with fire, and then there was just black.

I woke up hours later, still laying on the dock, but when I opened my eyes, the colors were so intense, it almost hurt too much to fight keeping them open. My head pounded. I have never felt so disoriented. I managed to pick myself up and I struggled to keep my balance as I headed back

22

Ashley Greathouse

towards my car. With squinted eyes I looked up the path and that is when I saw him.

Shit! How long has he been there? I thought to myself before trying to think of explanation in case he had witnessed something he should not.

"Well, here we are again Goddess of Darkness," he said to me as though we were reuniting. I could not help but show a slight emotion of weakness, confusion, and fear. I did not like this feeling he gave me. "I really didn't think it would take you this long. You almost had it when you were little, but at least you were able to come to me matured." His last words were said with a seductive smile, and he reached out to me as if I would come running into his arms.

I was not ready to admit that I had no memory of him as he hinted that I should. I feared admitting that would be admitting defeat. I really was not expecting the return of my powers to not come with the ability or knowledge of how exactly to use them, not to mention so much pain.

I had plans, and this was not worked into them. I could feel my power now more than I have ever felt anything, but I could also feel how unstable it was. Like a baby, my power needs to crawl before it runs. I cannot chance losing control, ending the world, and having my powers locked away again. I fear a second time of revoking would be a bit more permanent. I must think fast.

"And are you ready to be my Dark Prince?" I asked

23

coyly, playing along as much as I could.

He burst into uncontrollable laughter and in a flash stood just inches away from me. "Rebecca, my love, your humor is, without a doubt, everything I hoped it would be. We have never been formally introduced. However, you have been my Goddess of Darkness far before you were ever created.

"You're the beginning to my end, and Grace's last efforts to keep you from me would have always played out in vain. It was up to you, when and how you would unlock what was keeping you from me. I gave Grace her power, though your family praised God for his blessing.

"In a way, they were right to pray, but I am not the God they thought they were rejoicing, and my intentions were purely selfish. I can assure that much. See, I needed you to suffer, I needed you in the dark about who you were, and I needed Grace to do so by taking away every chance you could possibly have had to do the right thing. If you regained your powers because they were stripped and hidden from you like a dirty secret, I knew that you would be damned. All I had to do was get Grace to believe she was doing what was right…"

Confusion flooded my mind and before I could think, I was already blurting out my reply. "Couldn't you have just let everything be? Let the universe take its course! I can understand gifting a human family a witch so there would be ties to a bloodline for my powers, but why make me suffer? Look what I've done!" I pointed back towards the lake, stained with the blood of my victims.

"You're telling me there were other ways I could have unlocked my powers?" At this point I was shaking with rage. "You made me a kil…"

"NO!" he bellowed at me. "YOU made yourself a killer, Rebecca. You chose this path. You searched for your answers and jumped at the first thing you stumbled on. You had so many opportunities, so many different paths." He patted my head and then placed his hand under my chin, lifting my head to gaze into his breathtaking blue eyes. "I'm not displeased by your choice, my love, my Goddess. I am displeased with you regretting your actions. If bringing death was not your nature, wouldn't you have refused this path?"

His question haunted me. *He is right.* I did not question the path that led me here. I did not attempt to look for another way or hesitate in slaughtering the one hundred souls needed to unlock what is mine. From my first kill to my last, they were all as simple as slicing bread. I held no remorse to the innocent blood I spilled. "I enjoyed it…" I said, defeated.

"Of course, you did. You gave them peace that only darkness can bring. To you, to the real you, this was not a slaughter, this was the gift of eternal rest. Do you really think your words to Ruth, and so many of the others, were just words? They had truth and meaning behind them.

"Now, to answer your previous question. I did not give Grace her powers so you could belong to a bloodline. Rebecca, you are *THE Bloodline*. You would have existed without my meddling; you just wouldn't have chosen this path without first suffering."

"I don't understand?" I questioned.

He slumped his shoulders and put his index finger in the center of my forehead, and for the second time today, everything went black.

By the time I awoke again, I was inside my cabin. Alone. The air filled my nose with the overwhelming scent of cedar and dust. *Seems my senses are still heightened,* I thought as I sat up and rubbed my head. *At least my headache has eased a bit.* I looked around at the cabin which was mostly empty. It was only constructed to give off the illusion of a claimed property.

Other covens would see it as a mark of ownership and assume a human had claimed another part of nature for themselves. Witches are so content with their hiding and keeping themselves separated from the human world, that they would gladly surrender even the most sacred of places.

I was the beginning to his end? I questioned to myself as I tried to focus on everything that had happened. *Who is he?* I laid back down on the dusty plaid couch that smelled of neglect, trying to puzzle everything together.

The front door flung open and there stood the man from before. It did not hurt as much to focus in on him this time, and he did look like a modern-day God. He was for lack of a better words, perfect.

He just stood in the doorway, staring down at me. Most of the pain was gone, yes, but I was still so weak.

"That much power unlocking at once would kill most people, thankfully you're not a people." He smiled. "You're a goddess, reborn. Don't worry about losing control of your power either, it will be as easy to use as breathing, once you've rested that is." His voice was much softer now than before. He really had a way of coming off like he was comforting with his words and his unbreakable gaze that left me feeling desired.

"You keep calling me a goddess."

"Because that is what you are, my love," he said so factually. "Reborn, did you miss that?" he teased.

"I don't feel like a goddess and don't just tell me it's because I'm weak. I never felt like a goddess. Not before the ritual or after. What I have felt my whole life is pain. What kind of goddess can only feel pain?" I was done looking at this as a game of chess. There is no strategizing at this point.

If I want answers, *he* is where I will find them. And from how he is wording things, it is beginning to sound like he needs me to do something. *Seems like the ball is in my court no matter what, so I feel safe to let my guard down, at least a little.*

"You're right, you can let your guard down, and I do need you," he said, answering my inner thoughts.

GREAT, he reads minds. Awesome. "Just tell me what I need to know! It is not like we are in a story, and you need to keep building up for the big finish. Tell me who you are, what you want, and why you're insisting I'm a goddess," I spat out in anger.

"As you wish. My name is not important, but you can call me Shadow. I'm not a witch, and as I stated before,

I'm not a god that people would know."

Slowly, Shadow continued into the cabin, sitting beside me on the couch and patting my leg gently. "You see, you are the Goddess of Darkness, and I am the God of Shadows. We are, and have always been, connected. But where you have the power to both give and take life, by giving darkness or bringing someone back from it, I am only in control of what lies in the shadows of your darkness. And what I want is death.

"Woah. Wait just a minute here. You want me to kill you?"

I could feel my face beginning to flush. "Isn't there another god you could get to help you with this? Why go through all of this for me?"

"No, more like you're the last to show up to the deity party. You see. All the other gods and goddesses were created before any man or beast, but one goddess was to come and bring the end. That is, you, my love," Shadow laughed.

He continued, sensing that I wasn't exactly following. "You were created, in a sense, at the same time we all were created. But you were never gifted an immortal body. Instead, you were meant to be reborn into the world one day and fulfill your destiny and mine."

"I'm to bring the end of what exactly? The end of you? The world?" *I can feel that headache coming back, should goddesses even have headaches? I know he is in my head, but I cannot help but think he is trying to use me for a path I should not be on. This is not the plan I had in mind, especially if he is talking about ending the world. Though goddess is something I can work with.*

With confidence, I continued, "My plan was more to influence the world with my power until I was in control. In control of the New World Order, of everything. I was not going to hide in the darkness, and I was not going to continue with the factory setting we tend to constantly fall into. I was going to bring change."

My voice still trembled from being so weak, but the smug look on his face had me wanting this conversation to reach its end. "Now, what is with the constant reference to you being in love with me. If we have never formally met, how could I be your love?"

"I've waited for death before there was such an idea. After the creation of gods and man came the creation of witches, children of humans and gods. There began to be prophets born into this universe, and a being such as I learned to pass the concept of time by listening.

"This world would bare the Goddess of Darkness, bringer of the end. But this goddess would fall stray from her path, and much like the world, she would grow fond of its inhabitants."

I cut Shadow off. "So, I was never meant to bring the end?"

He sighed, "No, you were. However, just like humans, gods have freewill as well. At least we do to a degree. From the first Visioned Witch, I learned on your falling stray from your task. That you would undoubtedly keep the shadow of time alive. You see, despite the New World Order group you seem so fond of controlling, and the world itself, there are more forces keeping me here and those same forces play a valuable role in what could possibly change your path.

"The humans call him the Sun, witches know him as a god, but I promise you he's far more sinister than even the one you all refer to as the Devil.

"He is everywhere there is life, keeping it in a never-ending cycle. What dies gets replaced, what lives becomes dependent, what becomes dependent falls victim. He slowly sucks the energy from everything his light touches and holds them, as well as me, prisoner with his rays. I am trapped. We all are. So, would you not love the only being that could free you from your torture?"

"So, you expect me to end the world by casting eternal darkness because of the Sun? For you? Look, Shadow, you manipulated my life. All to end your own. The prophecy said I fall from my path, and my great-great-aunt did everything to keep me from my path. Did it ever occur to you that your meddling is what changed my mind? That putting me through pain and suffering was the motivation I needed to form an alliance with the Sun? Prophecies are tricky; not even a god can decipher them because the future is ever-changing. Always."

I stormed outside, *back to my special place*. No, *to my car*. I need to get as far from this creature as I can. Time to get back on track. Shadow is on his own. I pulled open my car door and got inside. One hand on the ignition, the other ready to cut the wheel and speed off.

Finally, something was back on course for me. I

turned the key and filled myself with so much excitement as the engine roared up. All I could think about was getting home, and in a blink, I was there. *I teleported? Now, this is a preferred means of transportation.* My inner thoughts rejoiced.

Oh, but my car! I rushed to my front window and was relieved to see my black metal steed resting in the driveway. I turned around to head down the hall to my study when Shadow came around the corner. *Fuck...*

He walked over to my island bar that separated my living room and kitchen and pulled out a stool to take a seat. He did not say anything, just motioned for me to join him. My face is bright red with a tornado of emotions. Hesitantly, I walked over to the island. Instead of taking a seat, I walked around to the other side to face him. His eyes met mine with so much fury. His once calming gaze was now clouded with anger.

"Rebecca. Do not make me an enemy."

We stared at each other for a long time before I dared to speak, but before I could, my leather sofa was consumed in flames.

"I warned you that I was more than a witch, more than just any god. Did you really think I was less than powerful?"

"I didn't care!" I spat the words at him. "Here is a shocker for you. I've read of the prophecy you wish I'd comply with. Not interested!" The fire had moved to the carpet, walls, and ceiling. I lifted my hand and waved it, snuffing out the flames as if they never existed. "You're not the only powerful thing in this room. Did you forget, Shadow, that my power trumps all that has been or will be? So yes, I do see you and everyone as less than."

He took a long deep breath, "No, it's the only part of the prophecy I fully counted on." He gestured for me to look back out the window, but it was too dark to see anything. Wait. It is three in the afternoon, why is it so dark?

"What did you do!" I screamed. His answer did not matter. I knew it was not what he had done, but what I had done out of blind anger and a cocky attitude.

"Thank you," he whispered as he faded into the darkness.

I rushed to the window and watched in horror as the glass began to fill with a thick coating of ice.

He manipulated me.

When I snuffed out the flames, all I could think about was proving my power and getting rid of the fire.

I could see my breath in the air.

And then the power went out.

All that was left was darkness.

I destroyed the sun.

Where Memories

Are Made

What makes a friendship? What are the building blocks needed to set a foundation that will last forever? Is it kindness... Lord, I hope it's not? I hope for everlasting bonds that was forged by something huge. But is kindness not a big deal? Not really, not if you ask me. Kindness is never without reason. No one does nice things without some sort of expectation that will follow their selfless act. Kindness is evil hidden with a smile. Oh, you don't believe me? Then allow me to introduce my favorite group of *kindhearted* friends who are responsible for why I've drawn up such conclusions.

Hidden in the darkness, I watched these three girls grow to become the picture-perfect idea of what companionship looks like. Since grade school I watched Nikki, Crystal and Sarah become the best of friends. And I can assure you that innocent kindness had nothing to with it. Still, each of them came together through something that started out so small, but this small 'thing' quickly grew into something quite large.

But can we really blame them? At first, that's exactly how I viewed it. How could I blame them for being the way they were, for having 'things' that needed to be protected. Secretly I wanted more than anything to share a small 'thing' with them too. Unfortunately for me, I had nothing small or big to offer to their list that bonded them so strongly. I was nothing more than a boring rural child, unlike them; and did they ever find so much joy in reminding me of that.

Still, I longed for their friendship. See, when you

grow up surrounded by more trees than buildings, you'll befriend just about anyone who might help you make the best out of country-living. It's either that, or you become that weird kid who talks to their neighbor's dairy cow. No one wants to be the weird kid. Everyone, however, wants friendship. So, I waited for an opportunity to be a part of what they had.

Here I am now, well past the age where one should continue to chase after childhood friendships. And here they are, proving that their 'thing' has stayed with them well into their adult life, making them an unstoppable trio. Obviously, they have shared in all the major celebrations in their life, from graduating from college, building families, and all the way to pursuing careers. I must admit, finding out their bond is so strong brings me comfort, even though I know the dark truth of how they've clung so tightly together. Now, I'm even more pleased to see them returning to the place where it all started. The place where memories are made. The place where 'things' either build or sever friendships.

As the person who was only ever a watcher to them and not someone who was a part of their world, I got to witness all the highlight moments from the nosebleed section, that was the treetops. If I wasn't going to be given a chance to join them, then I was at least going to watch them...

Their time growing up was always spent exploring these woods together, so it was easy to spy on them, if that's the label we're going to go with. But spying was never my intention. I honestly just wanted to live through them, even if it wasn't firsthand experiences. I watched them though, as they pushed as deep into the woods as they were willing to go, which wasn't very far at all. Still, I watched them build what they would dub as their kingdom.

In truth, it was nothing more than a bare spot, one that was perfectly hidden by the surrounding trees and thick overgrowth. There they built a cute little fort out of sticks and dug out a small fire pit where they would gather around nightly, telling scary stories while roasting marshmallows until midnight. Then came the teenage years. The fun time where you learn to adapt to new beginnings.

This group did not just flow into young adulthood though; instead, they welcomed it with open arms, quickly making their spot even more of a kingdom by inviting all the townies in for the hidden festivities. I'm sure that sharing their cute little campsite made them feel more like queens than anything… at least at first.

Soon it became painfully obvious that they started to feel like their kingdom was being overthrown. Without their consent, more and more kids that they did not know, started to show up. As nature will have it, in the cold and cruel world of teen spirit, they found themselves no longer welcomed to the very spot that they had founded and built so many memories, causing them to be out of sight for me, but not forgotten. Some 'things' you just can't forget.

It is funny how some people can bury memories away, while others like myself remember so strongly. Watching them all together now, it was clear that each of them have decided to allow their memories of certain 'things' to become smothered by the new memories they have made away from this place. If they hadn't, then they wouldn't dare come back here.

I stayed silent, watching them as I have always done, hidden by the trees. Nikki was the first to show up to the now empty field that once was the location of her childhood home. Steadily she parked her rusted CJ7 and jumped down from her chariot made of solid steal. I recognized her immediately. The way she stared off in the direction of where her home used to be… I instantly verified my hunch.

The only thing that took me by surprise was the fluffy husky that followed her out of the jeep and the teenaged boy who slumped out of the passenger side. Nikki never struck me as the family type, yet here she was, suburban pet and all. I rolled my eyes at the sight. The girl I knew was far too selfish for a busy family life. Afterall, she made it her mission when she was young to run from the family she did have.

I kept my eyes on her, admiring her strength as she began putting the heavy cloth top back on the Jeep, stopping just for a moment to shoot daggers at the son who offered no assistance. There was also the adorable way she pushed herself not to look back at the sight that was more than likely triggering more memories than she bargained for. *What brought you back here, Nikki?*

Of course, I started to figure it out once I learned that the boy could not only ignore his mother's struggle, but also complain at the same time. *What a show this is turning out to be*, I thought smugly.

"Mom, we're really going to camp here?" he scuffed, looking out into the wood line.

Fastening the last strap and securing the Jeep's top, Nikki sighed, "Not out here. Back there." She pointed with her head before wiping her hands down the front of her shirt. "I suppose getting a little dirty is going to inevitable."

"Awesome," her son said with so much sarcasm that I nearly laughed myself off the tree branch.

This is absolute gold.

Growing up, Nikki was always the first one in the group to shoot me down with so much snark that it was borderline cruel. To see her getting a taste of her own medicine, from her own child at that. Well, I could almost die and go to heaven... almost.

"Thomas, why don't you tie up Lou up to the hitch and get him some water?" Nikki instructed, not bothering to hide her annoyance.

"Yeah, come on Lou. You want some wat..." Thomas was taken aback by Lou's sudden change in attitude. Just moments ago, the dog was friendly, but was now fixated on the tree line, growling, and barring his teeth as he looked right at me. "Mom, something in the woods has Lou spooked. Is that seriously where we're going to camp at?"

Nikki stormed over to the back of the Jeep, snatching Lou's water bowl from inside as she made her way. "My God, he's a city dog, T. He's smelling all kinds of different scents right now. Animals fear what they don't know just like humans." She bent down, patting the dog's head until he was back to his old friendly self. "See T, he's fine. And for the last time, yes. We're ca-amp-ping."

"Whatever you say, mom. I still think we should have left him with the neighbor. Or, I don't know, not came at all. You and the aunties have the dumbest ideas sometimes."

"Oh yeah, we'll see how dumb this is when the twins show up," she snapped back.

"Ha! More like, how will it be once 'Tragic Tracy' shows up?"

"THOMAS!"

"What?! She's such a buzzkill."

"A buzzkill? Really? And how would you know what a buzz even is 'Mr. all my friends are online?' Are there codes now that get you wasted?" She laughed before a car made its way down the dusty road ahead. "Speak of the devils... I really hope Sarah and the girls don't mind that we brought Lou." Nikki looked down to the elder dog who was chewing his anxiety away on a stick.

Thomas began to quickly adjust his shirt and smooth over his hair that was frazzled by the ride to the old homestead. "Like I said, we should have left him at home. I'm not watching him the whole trip either. You drug me here to have, how did you put it? To have fun? Well, I can't really have fun while taking care of a big old baby that's scared of everything."

"Well, he needs to have *some* wildlife experience in his days," Nikki said to herself, more like she was practicing her defense for when Sarah blows a gasket over the wannabe wolf.

A black SUV, now covered in dust, eased in beside the Jeep. The windows were jet-black, and the vehicle was completely decked out in chrome. The driver opened their door. I could tell that Nikki was expecting Sarah to pop out, but low and behold, another new face. The woman was far too old to be a child to Sarah, and she dressed like she was an FBI agent.

I wonder who she is?

Following the mysterious woman, the passenger door burst open and out jumped this extremely high-energy man. He was older than the mysterious woman, but he had more life to him than the young man who I had been watching evade any sort of responsibility. *Now this guy, this guy is interesting.* Without warning he reached back into the SUV, pulling out a giant brown duffle bag which he immediately began to rummage through until grabbing out the biggest camera I have ever seen and attaching an even bigger lens to the front.

The mysterious woman demanded my attention as she swiftly opened the back door to the SUV, extending her hand and welcoming two beautiful girls to the empty lot. It took my mind a moment to adjust to the level of perfection that radiated from them. *No wonder Thomas was sprucing himself up.* But then Nikki rushed past the gathering group, nearly knocking Thomas over as she wrapped her arms around the two beauties.

"Oh my gosh, you girls, I've missed you so much! Where's your mom?" Nikki was bobbing her head from side to side looking for her best friend, refusing to let the two girls go, or breathe.

Hmmm… Maybe they haven't been as close as I thought.

At this point, I was starting to have some fun just trying to guess who was who and what all I've missed in re-maining the girl who never left her childhood home. I was certain this vehicle and twins belonged to Crystal. There was no way I could be wrong; she was always so over-the-top, and of course, that would never change.

"Nikki, you better let them girls go before Nadia over here has a meltdown," a posh voice called from inside the SUV before a dainty leg emerged from the backseat. Crystal slowly slid out, apparently' not requiring the same assistance her daughters needed. Nadia, who was the mys-tery woman, was on high alert as she shot Nikki a look that pierced like daggers. Crystal soothed her companion, "It's okay, Nadia. This woman would never mess with our star beauty queens. Besides, you knew who all would be here…"

Nadia seemed to relax a little, but she still seemed tense as her gaze fell to the dog who matched her anxious demeanor.

So, she's a bodyguard, huh. This just keeps getting better and better.

Nikki broke the silence, "So, who is Nadia? I didn't think we could plus one. This was supposed to just be us girls and the kids." Her voice held a sarcastic tone, showing that she was still the same spiteful girl I knew long ago.

"Nadia is Tiffany and Makayla's assistant, driver, stylist, and personal bodyguard, and of course we would need to bring her for the photo shoot," Crystal emphasized, adding a pleading wink, hinting that Nikki should not expose the illusion she had up her sleeves.

"So why is Auntie Nik here?" the girls asked in unison, breaking free from her clutches, and moving over to where Nadia stood.

"Well, I decided it would be nice to have some company, plus safety in numbers, right?" Crystal nervously laughed through her response.

Is that fear I sense? Surely rich and spoiled Crystal hasn't allowed anyone but herself to be in charge of her life?

"Yeah!" Nikki added, "Plus Sarah would have to be here since she owns all of this and is paying for your photoshoot. Not to mention, no one knows these woods better than your mom and aunties." Crystal smiled at Nikki, thanking her for continuing the charade.

"Speaking of plus-ones, what is this?" Nadia scoffed pointing at Lou, who was just watching everyone with a nervous wagging of his tail, waiting patiently for the tension to fade.

If Crystal's eyes had lasers, Nikki would be dead. *Dog drama?* But before anything else could unravel, another car zoomed down the dirt road and skidded to a stop just a few feet away, completely breaking up the hostile moment between friends.

Here she is… The woman of the hour, Sarah.

Aggressively the passenger door flew open and out jumped a young teenage girl who was dressed like she was a CEO. She stormed to the backend of the car, looking back with so much anger as she jerked her sunglasses from her face and starred in disbelief as Sarah exited the driver's seat.

"Hey everyone!" Sarah said, never letting her smile disappear and ignoring the fueled-up teen of hers.

Crystal steadily walked towards Sarah, pulling her in for hug and giving Sarah an opportunity to quickly whisper something in Crystal's ear. I wasn't certain of what was said, but the way Crystal averted her eyes from Tracy made it obvious that there was more going on.

I moved my gaze to read Nikki, and her demeanor was the same. A mixture of shame and remorse... *Interesting.*

But then Nikki shocked me. She took the tension-filled moment and turned it around. "So, who is ready to get this show on the road?"

The flamboyant man joined in on the notion, "Yeah, we should probably get going, a few more hours and I'll have the perfect sunlight to capture some phenomenal photos of these two beauties!" He smiled over at the twins who were looking very confused, but quickly changed their attitude the moment they were brought back in for the spotlight they obviously craved.

I watched as the group took turns helping each other gather supplies and begin to head towards the tree line, moving closer and closer to me. Well, all except for Tracy and her mom. While the group made their way towards the old kingdom of theirs, the two of them stayed behind to put on quite a performance.

Sarah initially waved her friends on, nodding her head back towards the upset young lady, hinting that there was a private discussion that needed to take place before they could rejoin the group.

"Okay, Tracy, what is with this display?" Sarah turned and snapped once everyone was out of earshot, or so she thought.

"My dad's business is not a joke, Sarah! You cannot just tell the board you are doing one thing then plan a reunion at the company's expense; it is not right! If you wanted to do this, you should have planned it before this entire area was a company liability! Do you understand the risks here? What if one of them burns the whole place to the ground?"

Sarah moved her hands to her temple, attempting to rub away the stress, "Tracy, you're overreacting. And look what you've done once again!" She motioned her hands to the woods. "You've made yourself appear to be a spoiled brat who is throwing, yet another, temper tantrum."

"But…" the girl responded, sounding uncertain of herself now.

Sarah held up her hand to cut her off, "Shh," she said, motioning for the two of them to sit back in the car. "Let's talk in here, okay?"

Damnit. I cannot hear now, I thought as the slow flames of rage began to burn deep inside me as I continued to give the two of them my full attention. I could not make out anything, but I could still see movement.

It was obvious that the young lady had begun to cry and Sarah was right there to console her, offering some tissues and a bottle of water before exiting the car once again. Only this time she left the young girl behind, grabbing out a small travel bag from the backseat and then making her way to rejoin the group.

It was a rather annoying dilemma. On one hand, it appeared as though Tracy was Sarah's stepdaughter, and not biological. But on the other hand, it was not uncommon for a child to call their parents by their given name out of spite. Still, I was certain that Sarah is the one responsible for buying up this entire rural town just to tear it done and build empire of farmland.

I do have to admit, when the first bulldozer showed up and tore down Nikki's old house, I was a little thrown back. As that day progressed, however, and more and more cranes, tractors, and dump trucks started to show up it became clearer at what was really going on. Plus, blue-collar workers sure do love airing out the laundry of their overseers. But this, seeing the little bitch show up here, in person, after everything she's done? This was the icing on the shit-cake she baked.

It was hard for me to remain so calm as I watched her walk through the woods alone. At any moment, I could have swooped down from the treetops and ended her right there. But I wanted her to know my pain, my confusion. I want her to admit to all the 'things' she's hid.

Sarah made it to the group, and she looked so pleased, giving them all that smug smile that she intended to come off as comforting and warm. She started to apologize and explain Tracy's behavior, but the way she did it… it was so condescending and at the poor child's expense. The girl had such a valid stance, but each one of them seemed to share Sarah's outlook on the outburst.

"You know, I'll go back and sit with her. It's a long hike when you don't know the area. She could be alone for longer than she realizes," Nikki said, adding a fake smile that pleaded for Sarah to deny the gesture.

And just like when they were young, the intention was not just picked up on, but thanked. "That is sweet, Nikki, but I agree with Sarah. Tracy is probably more embarrassed than anything, and alone time could be her way of dealing with it. You don't want to impose on someone's coping mechanism," Crystal interjected.

They were really a sickening bunch, constantly looking out for each other's lies and manipulations. None of their kids seemed a bit shocked and the two accompanying adults didn't even question it.

But I did. And for good reason.

I didn't stick around to eavesdrop on the exchange of excuses and coverup. Instead, I took my opportunity while they were all distracted to introduce myself to Tracy. Something that I had already planned to do, though our original way of meeting was meant to go a little different. Regardless, I was met with the outcome I was aiming for, with every person here.

Tracy was dead.

I wasn't surprised. Honestly, this all might work out even better than I expected. I looked around the car, noticing the bottle of water Sarah had handed Tracy. The poor thing was still clutching it. *Poison.* It was such a played-out method and yet it was almost poetic that it would happen again at the same spot where Sarah poisoned two others.

Well, where Sarah, Crystal and Nikki poisoned two others.

I wonder, are they all here to off their own kids? I debated if I should just return to the trees and let nature take its course, allowing the group to simply lower their own numbers. But I knew that was not how they operated. All of this was premeditated by the three of them. There was no way it wasn't, and I could almost bet that I know exactly what they're up to.

I rushed back to the cover of the treetops, ready to make my first move and I was right on time to a perfect opportunity.

The hyper twins were running around, striking different poses against the tree that surround the still barren secret circle that housed so many memories. They were oblivious to what they were celebrating. "This spot is lowkey amazing, Tiffany!" one of the girls squealed to her sister.

"Right! But I think Aunt Nikki said something about a lake?" the other twin responded.

Nikki let out a strong laugh, "Oh you girls, don't put this on me. For all I know, Aunt Sarah over here has already destroyed it with her attempt to grow weed."

"For the love of GOD. My husband would roll in his grave if I used his money for pot! For the last time, Nikki, it's hemp and it's completely legal to grow."

Crystal joined in on the teasing, "I'm sure he's been doing nothing but rolling in his grave."

"Like you want our dad to do?" one of the girls

snapped.

"Makayla!" Crystal gasped.

Her daughter just held her gaze.

"Okay, how about we find this secret lake?" The photographer timidly intervened, "The sun will set soon, and this is why we're here, right?"

"Right… which is why I'm going to ask why there's a dog here? Crystal, these girls cannot risk being put in danger," Nadia quizzed, her eyes glued to Nikki. "Honestly, I'm feeling like you three are up to something that doesn't really add up. Why are any of you here?"

Nikki took a deep breath. "Okay, you caught us. Look, Nadia, is it? We're all friends, close friends, except for you and whoever in the hell silk-shirt dude is. Crystal let us know that the girls needed an outdoor shoot for their brand, and well, this spot is the perfect place for that. Plus, we could all get together, with our kids, and build some new memories at our old spot. Sue us, I guess, for being corny moms. And my dog isn't going to do shit, so back off already."

Nadia took a few steps forward, causing Nikki to step back a bit and everyone else to stop in their tracks. "Back off? With all due respect, these girls are my top priority. So, no. I'm not going to back off. If your dog makes a single move, dead." She opened her jacket to reveal her gun holstered snuggly against her waist.

Sarah quickly stepped between them, "Okie dokie. So, the lake is still here. Private property owned by a fearsome woman who really did a number on my legal team."

She let a nervous laugh slip, "I might not be able to buy it, but I'll gladly tell you where it is."

Crystal stepped over to Nadia. "The woman never visits… and I wouldn't bring my kids to a place that would put them in danger." She looked up and into Nadia's eyes. "I'm not their father…" she spat before turning around to the pile they had gathered their luggage into. "If you girls want to explore, go. It's about a 5-minute hike that way." She pointed, now lowering her head, and looking defeated.

"Well, now we have it. Shall we?" the man asked the girls.

"Ummm, yes," they cheered in unison as they followed the man towards the trail their mom had pointed to.

Nadia adjusted her jacket, switching her line of sight between Nikki and Crystal.

"Nadia…" Crystal stated, still looking down at the ground. "You need to learn your fucking place," she growled from clenched teeth.

"Yes ma'am."

So much hostility.

This was good, too good. I watched the group as they sat in silence. Thomas, who has stayed quiet the whole hike in, was finally doing something and helping his mom set up the tents. But Sarah and Crystal just sort of watched. It was rather boring really. But I guess there isn't a whole lot the three could discuss freely with Tomas still hanging around. Which was fine; guess this is my cue.

I cautiously moved around their camp site and headed in the direction the other party members went.

Sarah is right about the owner being fearsome… But like anyone would honestly abandon their property without some sort of protection. Unlucky for these four though, since the guard dog has been watching them the whole time.

I could not help but laugh at the misfortune that I was about to unleash on them.

The four made their way through all the thorns that grew as sign of caution, but the well-prepared bodyguard was ready for almost anything it seemed. She worked at forging a path with a machete she had holstered to her calf until they had finally reached the lake.

"Oh my, it's beautiful. And what an adorable cabin!" the photographer announced as he admired the scenery.

"Why are we sleeping in tents if there is a cabin, Max?" Tiffany snapped.

"No kidding? What the hell!" Makayla agreed as both looked to Nadia for an answer.

"Why don't we head back to camp and ask?" Nadia insisted. It was obvious that she relished in any moment the girls would have reason to question their mom. "My money is on the damn dog being a deal breaker for the owner of the cabin."

"What do you have against dogs?" Makayla teased.

"Sis! Stop!" Tiffany added, "We both know that Nadia was attacked by a deadly man-eating toy poodle when she was a kid." They both boomed with laughter, leaving Max snapping his camera, making no waste of their realistic smiles and emotion.

I could see that Nadia wasn't as well respected as she

hoped.

No wonder she wants them to hate their mom. She wants to be the one they like more. Jokes on you lady. Those two are spawns of Crystal; they won't ever respect themselves let alone someone else. Without wasting too much time gawking at how evil clearly breeds evil, I lowered myself down from the treetops and moved in for my first strike of the evening.

Without warning I brushed my nonexistent hand across both the unknowing twin's backs. Being a ghost had it perks, but being a ghost gifted with darkness from the most badass deity there is… priceless. Keeping people away from this area was a job I was happy to do, especially since he promised that I'd get my moment of revenge.

There wasn't a lot I could have done to them had I remained a helpless lost soul, too focused by hate to crossover. But as a remaining soul with powers, I can and will, dominate those who wronged me and shortened my life. Infecting those two with just a sliver of my darkness was a rush I wasn't aware I could still feel.

Now, all I must do is wait on that moon.

I took my leave and headed back to the three I really wanted, eager to see their reaction to the gift I just gave them. Nikki and her son were finishing up the last tent and Crystal and Sarah seemed to have made some use out of themselves and built a roaring fire. I nestled myself back in a cozy position in the trees and ate my metaphorical popcorn as I waited for my efforts to play out.

"I guess I'll take Lou and check on Tracy. Maybe that will help a bit when the others get back, and by others, I mean that witch of a bodyguard you and your husband found," Nikki said as she hammered the last stake into the ground, securing the tent in place.

"I'll do it..." Thomas huffed. "I need to clear my head anyway. You all are always so much drama when you get together," he teased with a coy smile.

"Oh really?" Sarah joked back, "And here your mom said that you weren't a real Tracy fan."

He smiled nervously, "She's just a little much with her walk-a-straight-line attitude is all. But thanks to you, I've grown up around her. She's like a sister."

"Like a sister, huh? Like my girls?" Crystal pipped in.

Thomas's face turned bright red. "Seriously, mom! You have to repeat everything, don't you?" He grabbed Lou's leash, untying it from the tree trunk and started back towards where the cars were parked. "I didn't expect she'd pout this long," he addressed, attempting to change the subject before the twins came back and overheard.

"Okay, well, take a flashlight. By the time you two get back it will be pitch black in these woods," Nikki said, handing her son an oversized lantern.

"Thanks mom, I think I'll be able to see two states over with this thing." He laughed, taking off with the dog into the woods.

Alone at last.

"What is taking them so long?" Crystal started to complain as she took a twig and knocked off some of the fungus that was growing on the log they had strategically placed years ago.

"Oh, they'll be back… Thomas soon enough too, once he finds Tracy," Sarah said so matter of a fact.

"Like I said, you're paying for his therapy. He really pretends to dislike her, but the truth is, this is going to destroy him," Nikki responded.

"I can't believe how many years it's been and we're still killing off people like this is a game of chess," Crystal added.

"Is that really why you had to lie to get your kids here? Secretly you believe one of us would just off one of your family members without going through you first? Seriously, Crystal. Get off your high horse or whatever pills you are popping now. Whatever it is, paranoia was never your color," Nikki spat.

Crystal pushed herself up. "You know what, maybe it was!"

"That's fucking rich, coming from the girl who killed my parents without as so much as a head's up first," Nikki snarled.

I honestly couldn't take any of it anymore. "Should we all tell our story of death?" I said from above them.

"What the fuck was that?" Sarah said, jumping up and pushing her back up against Crystal's.

"Shit." Nikki said, twirling around trying to find my location, "I thought you killed her already?"

"Nikki, that's not Tracy's voice!" Sarah exclaimed.

"Ouch!" I blurted. "None of you remember me. Now that really stings. Especially because I remember all of you."

"Who the fuck are you?" Crystal demanded, "You better stay away from my girls!"

"Your little devil pups? Oh, they're just fine. In fact, I think they're getting ready to take a break and have a little snack."

Subtly, but not out of my sight, Sarah tapped against Crystal's arm. "It's Pam," she whispered.

"Good. You do remember," I rejoiced sarcastically.

"PAM!" Nikki blurted out.

I looked up at the moon that was starting to ascend into the sky. "We'll have to finish our little talk later. I think those cute little puppies of yours are still hungry. I'd run... if I were alive anyway."

They did not hesitate, at least Sarah and Nikki didn't. Crystal though, she was always full of surprises as a kid, and here she is now, still as shocking as ever.

"You choose death so soon?" I asked her.

Still frozen in place, she let out a wounded response, "I didn't want to see you dead, you know."

"I know. You just wanted your secrets to die. From the looks of things though, Crystal, all you have done is continue to create 'things' you need to keep secret. Like, your friend's bloodlust for money."

"Am I who you blame then? Take me! Leave my girls out of this!" she begged.

"I blamed you at first, but I also sympathized with you all too. That's the irony here. When I found out that you killed off Nikki's parents so she could be a rich little snob like you, I was a little confused. But when I found out they covered up her uncle molesting her, I got it.

"See, I watched you all for a long time before I dared to reveal that I found you all out. In my head, it was supposed to go a little different. You all were supposed to help me too, like you did for each other."

"Help you? You literally blackmailed us and threatened to call the cops. What were we supposed to do?"

"Realize that I was acting just like you. You didn't appreciate the balls it took for me to even approach you three at all, especially after years of you all singling me out during church pitch-ins and school activities.

"What did you all think was going on? Really? You denounced the only other female child in this godforsaken shithole of a town and left me alone. No! You forced me to be alone. Guess who targets young girls who stay alone all the time, looking unwanted and unloved?"

"You were abused?" Crystal asked sounding shocked. "By who?"

"That doesn't matter now does it. Shit, even when I told you all who I wanted help getting rid of, all you focused on was hearing that I knew your secret. You three set me up and you didn't just kill me, you enjoyed it."

"Fuck." Crystal huffed, "The fucking preacher." She breathed out, sitting back down on the rotted log.

"Like I said, doesn't matter." We were interrupted by the howling of wolves. "Sounds like your kids are here."

Still, hidden away in the trees, I watched as the twin girls, now fully infected by the darkness that morphed them into the ravenous beasts they are now, slowly walked into the small clearing.

"Oh my god," Crystal managed to spit out as one of them dropped what was once Nadia's arm from their mouth and lunged towards their next prey.

I didn't stick around to watch the gritty part; I didn't need to. Just like the Old God had promised me, powers for revenge. All I had to do was keep people away, it was that simple. And if I remained an eerie feeling that spread deep through the surrounding woods, this day would come to me and with it, so would the wolves.

At the time, I wasn't sure what it all meant. I wasn't even aware of what exactly my powers were, not until I reached out and touched the girls. Then, it all made sense. It was almost like I could feel what I was doing, what I was infecting them with as I watched the darkness that consumes me tether out, leeching into their skin. Knowing that one day they would come back here, and I would be able to end them. It was enough for me to say yes, to become whatever it is I am now.

Still fueled by my need to kill the rest, I was suddenly hit with another overwhelming urge. I needed to find Max. For whatever reason, he had managed to flee from the girls as they were transforming. I could feel it, almost as if I were connected to the woods itself and could see everything that happened within it. Well, not really see, but know without knowing.

I didn't care much for what this need to find him meant, but it was almost like I was on autopilot at this point. I zoomed through the treetops until I had finally caught up to Nikki, Thomas, and Sarah. They were all huddled by the cars, unable to get any of them to start. A trick a put into place from the moment they arrived. Using the energy, I harnessed the vehicles to me to strengthen myself, all to watch them take their final breaths.

Originally, I had planned to pick them all off, one at a time. But now… now I'm overtaken by this urgency to find Max. To pass this power to him. I could feel myself fighting. It was either kill them now or find the next vessel and allow them to walk away. I couldn't let that become an option. They needed to die.

I pushed forward, too close to my goal to give up now. "I hope you all really didn't think I'd allow survivors?" I asked.

"Pam?" Sarah called out. "You need to stop this!"

"We- we… We didn't mean to kill you!" Nikki cried out.

"Mom! What is going on?" Thomas demanded, clearly shaken from everything that is happening.

"Poor boy, your mom and her friends are quite the little bunch of murderers. In fact, they even killed you!" I burst into an uncontrollable fit of crazed laughter as my darkness crawled its way down to Nikki, brushing caressingly against her cheek.

"No!" she screamed, unable to fight the infection I bestowed her.

Still, with each step she took towards her son, she fought against it.

"Nikki, what are you doing?" Sarah asked in fear,

stepping between her and Thomas.

"Now, now. Sarah, I thought you would be all in for team 'kill your kid'?"

"YOU killed Tracy?" Thomas spat out through tears, pushing past her and closer to his mom. "Mom, we need to go, NOW." He urged, dropping Lou's leash.

Bingo, I thought as my darkness coiled down once more, but this time landing the dog as its target. And just like that, I could feel that my part of the deal had been completed as I was sucked back into the trees that linked me to this world.

I could hear Nikki and her dog's skin began to tear, as the infection spread through their entire being, transforming them into wolves forged from darkness. But none of it mattered to me anymore; I couldn't even find peace in hearing Sarah's screams as she and Thomas were ripped apart limb from limb. There was no sense of accomplishment, just a longing to move on to my next task.

The shocking realization hit me and hit hard: I had been used. Not for what I wanted to do, but for what I was going to do. For what evil I was storing until someone worthy crossed my path to take on the mantle of chaotic evil. Even in death, I'm nothing more than a replaceable soul.

I finally found the sad sack of meat that was to be my successor. He was balled up in a briar bush, crying quietly and praying to any god who will listen. "Turns out, someone heard you."

"Please," he begged, refusing to even look where my voice had come from. "PLEASE, let me go."

"Yeah, apparently that's always been the plan, Max." I reached out, allowing my darkness to flow out of me. "Seems you have an eye for perfection, and that eye of yours is going to help him." Without any feeling of victory, I watched my darkness worm its way through every orifice in his skin…

… until I was nothing more than fading breeze.

The Perfect

Life

They say that if you work hard at something, you will eventually achieve it. I believed, and lived, that thought process every day of my life. I devoted everything to that notion. Of course, what I worked hard at was faking it until I made it. See, what I wanted to achieve was the perfect life equipped with the perfect house, perfect husband, perfect kids, and all the ins and outs that came with it. From an outsider's perspective, that is exactly what it appeared I had been blessed with. And I'd kill to keep it that way.

I was always so extra about everything too; so over-the-top. I would go as far as planning out evenings with my family - that were all just a charade. I would plan the perfect spot in the living room for a family picture, make sure everything that would be in the frame was perfect, pop in a movie (for a more believable background setting), and call for the kids. They knew the drill: smile for the camera.

As soon as the flash would fade my family would depart, not wanting to be around me for fear that I would demand a retake. They would each escape, leaving me to sit alone in silence. But I preferred that. I didn't need a distraction every five seconds stressing me out while I edited my photos. They needed to be perfect.

As soon as my heartwarming photos were ready for the public's eye to eat them up like apple pie, I would upload the darling moment with the kids to my many social media accounts. After that it was pour some wine and unwind as I sit and stare into my screen for the flood of approving likes and comments to eat up my battery life.

Oh, and my favorite pastime, I cannot leave that out. Submitting my perfectly captured moments to online photo contests; I lived for that. The thrill of how many likes I would receive was better than any drug, though I had not really experimented with anything of that nature. I mainly stuck with my fruity mixed drinks, the sweeter the better. And the taste of victory when I would win… it was divine.

Thanks to my online addiction, it did appear that I had so many accomplishments to be proud of. I had the perfect job at a corporate firm where I would bring home a nice weekly salary. My car was basically a computer on wheels - it was environmentally friendly too, with the price tag that screamed just how much you cared about the world. Then, for the cherry on top, my family and I lived in a historical two-story colonial home. It was absolutely the perfect home to own in Tennessee and I stopped at nothing to make it mine.

Our home sweet home that my family was caged in had giant white pillars that secured the porch, with soft blue shutters that hugged each window, and a gorgeous driveway that highlighted the landscaping as it curved back to the road that led down a steep hill and into the kingdom below. Of course, it was not an actual kingdom, not one that belonged to me anyway, but it was my view. I relished in my quiet mornings where I would sit on my porch, sipping my coffee, looking down at all the tiny little houses that sprinkled the valley's ground. In comparison to my home, all of those were garden sheds trying to pretend to be a suburban neighborhood.

While up high on our hill, we were surrounded by trees and wildlife, unlike our neighbors who had either a view of my house or their neighbor's siding. They were so clustered together; no wonder they all referred to this place as a castle. Once I discovered that fun fact, it was all the validation I needed for this to be my perfect home.

Our yard and flower garden were always trimmed and flowing with color, and our garage was a separate extension that matched the original home perfectly. Even with knowing there were no attached two-car garages that had an electric door built in the era of this house being constructed, still it blended in quite well. It should flow perfectly with the rest of the house though; after all, I paid a lot of money for it to be nothing but perfection.

So here it is, all that I am. A perfect mom, home keeper, and a force that was out of this world when it came to my career. But, despite me always having to be the perfect person at everything, I was not really one to travel. In my opinion, there is no way to really be "the perfect traveler," so it never interested me. On a vacation, every family gets treated like they are the best. It seemed like way too much effort to try and compete for MVP status when everyone is a winner, so I mainly kept to my online networks that were filled with everyone from my community, and I mean everyone.

I think I just wanted noticed, or maybe I just wanted so badly to hide the truth and live the lie, but the truth was that my house was not perfect. It took every penny I had to buy and restore this home, not to mention the second and third mortgage taken out just to keep up with appearances. My husband and I was in so much debt just trying to keep up. My car was leased, the children's clothes paid for with store credit cards, and that nice weekly salary was gone before it even hit our account.

We never threw events or dinners because part of being perfect was to also be mysterious. If I were to allow people in my home, the illusion would instantly die. We had three different floorings that made up the living room, but you would not dare see that in one of my photos. The life inside the home was just as much of a show as well.

How could I walk around so blind to what I had? How could I ever bring myself to be a better mom, wife, or person when I cannot escape the fear? I can't. There is a hollowness inside me now and there will never be anything to fill the void that once harnessed my heart and soul. Not to mention the regret that constantly overtakes my mind. *Oh God, what have I done?* All for the sake of my perfect image…

The only thing I have left of them now is my memories and social media posts but looking back at those only makes losing them so much harder. I would spend most of my time at my family's graves, just sitting in front of their tombstones, still playing out my role as the perfect mother. Only now my role was to cope exactly as a perfect mom would cope.

I was forced to play out this part and honestly, it was a natural role to play. Aside from the feeling like my chest had been ripped out and all I wanted to do was scream at the top of my lungs until I passed out, but you cannot be doing that if you are a perfect mom. What would everyone think? What would everyone say? I would quickly be labeled as a woman who lost her composure. Sure, many would reach out or show compassion, but that is not an option I had. I had to remain steady, calm, collected.

To help keep myself mentally in check I would find myself rethinking about that Monday morning. Trying to play just the memories of that day over and over in my mind. It was a day I will never let go of, but the days that followed will always haunt me in my dreams.

I had called into work letting them know I was too sick to come to the office. I never missed a day, that was just part of my perfect show I constantly had to put on. So, when I called in, I was instantly bombarded with get well soon emails, posts, and texts from my coworkers. I was so weak from the flu that I could not bring myself to reply or react to any of them. All I could do was lay in bed with my body wrapped in my fuzzy grey blanket with my TV remote at my side.

What came as a surprise that day was while resting was that I got to witness my family life like I was a fly on the wall. It was truly eye opening; I just wish it would have been enough to change me.

Ben, my oldest was getting his sister Brooke up and ready for school. I could hear the laughter echoing down the hall as he tickled her awake.

"You better start this day with a smile! Or else!" Ben said in his boogey monster voice. "Muahahahah!" he bellowed out as he grabbed her feet.

"I'm up! I'm up!" Brooke squealed between laughter. "I have an alarm clock you know!"

Ben mocked, "Sure, but does it make you laugh?"

That was a sound I had not heard often, my kids laughing.

Normally by this time, I am already at work, so they had no clue that I was still home. I was always the type that would show up to work 30 minutes early every day. I spend my mornings showing off my posts from the night before to my coworkers, soaking up their jealousy like it was what fueled me.

The moment Ben turned ten, I fell into this routine; he is seventeen now. Brooke is only four years behind him. I thought about how quickly they grew up, and how I had grown too selfish to enjoy it, or to see how perfect my kids really are.

The rest of their morning was spent downstairs. I could not make out what they were so happy about, just that every so often their giggles would reach my ears.

Robert, their father, was already at work by this time as well, living his dream of having a successful career. He was the CEO of his financial firm, so really his job was his home, and I did not see him much. My close friends would whisper gossip about him cheating on me, but I never played into it. As far as I was concerned, the money and stature were all that mattered.

When we first bought our house, it needed so much work, but there came a time when I stopped pushing for the minor remodels and started focusing on covering it up with the finest trending décor. We were far too busy to find contractors that would work on a historical home, so we fixed the outside ascetics and major issues then left it at that.

Now, I did not spend his money or even pay attention to his savings. All I paid attention to was the fact he paid his share of the utilities and contributing to the house. He never missed family photos, always looked happy, and helped keep the house running. After that, he was free to do whatever he wanted as far as I was concerned.

But if he were in town, Robert would be home in time to listen to the kids explain their day and get them tucked in for the night. He really adored them, and he was an amazing dad. Not a day went by that he did not make time to hear about their day. Sometimes it was done through webcam, but he made the time, nonetheless.

I cannot remember there ever being a time that I asked my kids how their day was. Much like with Robert, I honestly did not care about their escapades. They could commit murder and I would be more concerned with how they dressed while doing it. Thankfully, they were never in any trouble, they brought home good grades, and joined almost every sport and school event.

Ben had apparently taken Brooke to school this morning. I heard the car start up outside and Brooke yelling something at Ben about not playing dumb music before the car doors shut and they pulled away.

I kept myself busy if I could by working on some spreadsheets for a meeting I had tomorrow. Notifications for reminders going off every 10 seconds made it hard to think of anything else but work.

I could have gone to work this morning. Yeah, I had the flu, but I was not dying. It is just that something in me found it too much for myself to deal with today, so I stayed home.

I am so happy I did. All day I kept thinking about how sweet Ben and Brooke was to each other.

It is almost funny how that thought kept crossing my mind and how grateful I was to wake up feeling so sick. If it were not for me staying home, I would have never seen that my kids really were a perfect set of siblings, and I would have never entered their photo in that contest.

The contest was headlined, "The Sweetest Siblings," and the winners would receive an all-expense paid trip to a popular resort in Florida. The rules were simple: the siblings must live in Tennessee, must submit photo and story of why they should win this trip, they must be 13+ with at least one parent or guardian able to accompany them, among some other noticeably clear rules. It sounded PERFECT, for them at least.

There was no way I would make time to go with them. I had way too much to deal with at work. Not to mention that some of those rules would be simple for some, but for me, there is no way.

I knew Robert would go with them in a heartbeat. He was always looking for the next trip to take the kids on. They did enjoy camping, hiking, fishing... you name it. I did not hesitate; I uploaded a photo Robert had sent me from one of their trips to the contest. In this photo Brooke was pouring her water over Ben's head while he was making a goofy face - which was probably the reason for her pouring the water over his head in the first place. That much I had witnessed about the two of them, they were always teasing each other. Only I had always mistook it as bickering. It is just how they were with each other. I know that now, but now it is too late.

Too late to take back all those hateful stares, screaming at them to behave with my eyes. Too late to join in on their fun, to be a part of their inside jokes, or at least knowing what the joke was about. It is all too late.

I had submitted their photo along with an exaggerated version of this morning's events; how they were the sweetest kids and how they deserved to win. I honestly did not enter this contest for my own ego boost. I really wanted them to win.

Before I knew it Ben and Brooke were home. They sounded so happy. I could not help but feel proud that Ben took such great care of his little sister. I always assumed he would act like a typical teenager and force her to ride the bus, afraid to be seen with her. Not that Brooke was deformed or something. My children were walking poster kids for how you wish your kids looked. I was never jealous of their looks or charisma, instead I took pride knowing that I built those children up. They were always neat and tidy, decked out head to toe in name brands. Both took after me in appearance: tan, blonde, button noses and slender jawlines. Robert is the odd ball out with his dark hair, long nose, and deep brown eyes. The kids did take after him in the eye department though.

I heard the garage door open. I guessed that the kids were planning on riding bikes, that is about all that is in there, besides my car and the empty spot beside it for Robert's.

I bet they still did not realize I had taken the day off or that I was even home at this time. The next sound was the garage door closing followed by Ben's car starting back up, and car doors closing.

I could not help but feel they were trying to avoid me. Maybe they left something at school? That is what I would have believed, too, but I did not hear Ben's car return in the driveway until it was dinner time.

I had already dragged myself out of bed hours ago. I had finished going over my material for tomorrow's meeting; still sick or not, there was no way I was going to miss it. Not to mention miss cooking and posting a delicious meal I made for my family.

Tonight, it was tomato basil soup with homemade crescent rolls. I was still sick after all, so I needed to showcase a "trying to get better" meal.

Ben and Brooke came in just as I was snapping pictures of my beautifully arranged dinner display.

"I didn't know you were home today, mom. Were you here all day?"

"Yes, I wasn't feeling well and didn't want to get anyone one else sick. Would you be a dear and dim the light just a little, its reflecting off the soup way too much and ruining the photo." I really wanted to compliment them both on how much they impressed me this morning, but I was too consumed with my perfect image. I did not even care to bring up the two of them taking off instead of coming in to check on me when they realized I was home, or the fact I entered them in a contest. After the nausea faded, I was back to my old self and old ways.

Brooke beat Ben to it and dimmed the light as she walked through the dining room towards the staircase, avoiding eye contact, and most likely going to barricade herself in her room. She was always the last one to come down for anything, especially a photo, and only because I turned the Wi-Fi off.

Ben on the other hand was a peacekeeper. He was constantly trying to help me. I could not help but feel like his assisting me was just to speed up my nightly process so he too could disappear into his own life.

The rest of the week was a blur of repetitive days, but by Friday at 12 am, the results of the "Sweetest Sibling Contest" were posted. Over 6,000 entries were submitted, and I was tagged as the winner.

I could not believe it! The kind thought that gave reason for my entry, that started this whole thing, was quickly replaced in my mind with an overflow of selfish thoughts about being the best and having the best. I was so happy when my phone chimed and woke me up to that sweet sound of acceptance. I could not wait to tell the kids and Robert of their upcoming surprise vacation plans.

It was so hard to fall back asleep. I tossed and

turned for hours before finally giving up and started to prep for my good news instead. When it was finally a somewhat acceptable time, I rushed to wake up my family. After accomplishing my first task, it was time to bring everyone downstairs where I had a beautiful display of a breakfast food bar.

It really was stunning. I even had freshly squeezed orange juice and different choices of caffeinated beverages. They all stared at me, still in their robes, hair a mess, and not looking very picture worthy.

I found myself trailing off in thought of how to capture this moment without utilizing their faces, maybe just a photo of them holding hands? No. My thoughts interrupted by Robert growing impatient.

"Okay, Beth. What's the big surprise?" he asked while stretching out his arms above his head. He walked over to the counter and poured himself a cup of black coffee.

"Black? Really?" I thought as I witnessed him skipping past the cream and sugar options.

18 years of marriage and I never even knew how my husband took his coffee.

"Yeah, mom. I didn't have to be up for another hour, at least!" Brooke sounded even less enthused and more filled with resentment.

I have always chalked this up to a normal teenage girl's attitude but remembering how happy and kind she sounded with Ben, it made my heart ache that she was not that way with me.

"Okay guys. Here it is." I looked at Ben then looked at Brooke. "You guys won a contest that I entered you in called "The Sweetest Siblings"!" I explained prize, details, and the location. Their excitement well surpassed my expectations.

Brooke immediately started to send out texts of her winnings and plans of never leaving the spa.

Ben was amazed that the resort happened to have an amazing observatory, so all he could do was research what would be visible in the sky at that time.

Even Robert was on the phone putting arrangements for work into motion.

Robert paused, looked up at me with the most vibrant smile and asked, "Are your arrangements for work already done? Wow! You are excited for this; didn't you see the rule about no cameras or phones? I'm so happy you're still going to go!"

"No honey, unfortunately I can't attend." I went on about me being so behind schedule on closing some business deals and how I thought he would better benefit from the trip without me.

He seemed so sad that it almost made me want to change my mind. I did read the rules though, and there was no way I could sit through an entire weekend without my phone. I only do things I can instantly benefit from.

It was hard to see Robert so disappointed from my absence, but I had already started to envision plans of donating and blogging my helpful acts to the needy. Of course, I was using their vacation to still shine as a perfect person.

"Missing my family, so using this time away from them to help others #stayingbusy #cantwait #missthem," was the post I was planning on my accompanying my many photos of my cherished time with the less fortunate.

No doubt that would really make me stand out.

This weekend was spent stocking up on travel packs for the kids and Robert. New beach towels, sunscreen, and vacation outfits were bought, as well as road trip snacks.

By Monday, their bags were mostly packed and waiting in the foyer. The pre-vacation excitement had died down, and with old habits being hard to break, it was soon back to our typical weekly procedures.

Brooke seemed to be the only one that struggled with getting the week over with. All she could do was talk about the itinerary for Friday and how she could not wait.

The weekend retreat was to start off with a chauffeur picking up the winners at 5 am Friday morning, so come Friday at 3 am, my family was running around the house in a tornado-like fashion.

Though their bags were mostly pre-packed, they were still getting ready and gathering up last minute items to keep themselves occupied on the trip. No phones meant they really had to think about what to take.

Robert was scrummaging through the study searching for books he could read, Ben hunting for his old handheld game console, and Brooke organizing her sketch pad and colored pencils.

Finally, the car pulled up outside and the driver beeped the horn three times.

We were to ask the driver a security question to verify who he was, as well as verify the photo that was attached to the congratulating email and additional information pertaining to the trip.

Brooke, of course, was the first one to run out the door and head to the car. We all followed behind her and we were stopped by the driver holding out his hand.

"I can't let you in until we verify each other."

The security question also held another motive. Apparently, the winning family had to wear something that advertised for the funding company of the trip.

"There's always a catch," the chauffeur joked as he waited for someone to ask the security question.

We all laughed because we knew how corny they had made the question, because "the catch" he was referring to was, "Do you have any swag?" and the answer the driver was to respond with was, "You can have a shirt, hat, or flip flops – size nine."

Each chose the hat hoping it would be blown away, caught in the wind, but the driver assured them that he had plenty of extras, and he would be the one to accompany them the entire trip.

I took as many pictures of them departing as I could before the driver started to mutter comments about keeping to the schedule.

I allowed them to leave, stepping back towards the house, still clicking away photos. Slowly, the SUV faded down the hill out of view. I could not wait to edit these pictures, but unfortunately, they would have to wait if I wanted to still show up early to work. Of course, I did not want to break routine.

I spent most of my morning show off only the shots of my breakfast bar and photos of the family grabbing up their suitcases. Those were the only ones I was able to quickly edit from my car before walking into work.

The rest of my workday was filled with paperwork and other, sometimes overwhelming, work responsibilities. Today it was one of those overwhelming days.

Finally, I made it through my shift and back home.

Robert and the kids should well be in Florida by this time, but I would not hear from them until they checked into the resort.

Hours went by. I had already posted every photo of my family departing on their adventure and read every comment that was made, and still no word from my family.

"Did they forget to call?"

I would expect that at least Ben would call, knowing how furious I would be if I could not update my media posts with assuring words of their arrival and fun.

Comments were starting to trickle in now with people wanting to know if they made it okay.

"What kind of perfect mom doesn't know if her family is safe?" was what I instantly translated their comments to.

I could not take the suspense, or the judgement, so I called the resort myself.

The very chipper woman answered the phone with her scripted speech inviting me to join the fun today or book my stay.

I cut her off, not trying to seem rude, but trying to sound urgent. "Hello, my name is Beth Fields. My family won a trip to your resort, and I was just wanting to see if they've arrived?"

"Sure thing, Beth! I would be happy to help! What is the reservation under?"

I paused; I was not sure. That was never specified in the email.

I answered with several different names they may have used, the contest name, the company's name, my family's name, nothing showed up.

"I've worked all day, ma'am. Maybe describe them to me or the car they arrived in, and if you do not mind waiting, I'll ask around to see if anyone has seen them if I can't verify their arrival myself."

I described in as much detail as I could, waited on hold for 20 minutes and still nothing. I gave the receptionist my contact information so someone could notify me when my family made it in.

She insisted they may have somehow bypassed the check in desk or went straight to sightseeing. She was trying everything to comfort me and assure me they were fine.

Oh, how wrong she was.

I replied to the contact email I had received from the sponsoring company and immediately was sent an undeliverable message.

I had no other choice but to update my posts with as much information as I could with the ideas the receptionist had gave me. Trying to sound worried, but still confident in how much fun they were probably having.

"They wouldn't be teenagers if they didn't make you worry," one lady wrote.

"Sounds like my family!" teased another.

"Robert should know better!" exclaimed a common friend he and I shared.

Mostly it looked like I had appeased the commenters. An hour had passed without notification and then three chimed from my phone.

"Oh no, not more!" was all I could think.

I unlocked my screen; it was three different emails from the same contact that emailed me before with updated contest information.

No subject and nothing in the body of the email, just an attachment.

I clicked open the attachment, instantly my screen went blue, and then it was back to a normal blank document.

"Odd." I closed the document and responded with a similar email that I attempted before.

Same thing, an immediate undeliverable message replied.

It was late enough in the evening that most people would assume all was well with my family and that I had went to bed. I was safe from judgment, at least until morning, without having news of what my family was up to.

I sat around watching TV in bed for the rest of the night, volume of my ringer turned on high, and eventually I fell asleep.

I had set my alarm for an earlier time so I could call around to some hospitals and police stations. I had to have some kind an action put into play for a situation like this. At least I would have more information for social media.

I walked down the staircase that led directly to the kitchen.

I was told when this house was first built this section was used as the servant's quarters. I never really got too involved with the history of the house. I was more annoyed that its history caused so much headache when it came to remodeling, but I did like the extra staircase.

It was still dark outside, but I had no need to turn the lights on. Everything was always perfectly in its place. We had no pets, so there was no reason for things to not remain as we had left them. To my surprise, I stubbed my toe on something that was on the floor.

"Did we have an earthquake, and something fell?" I wondered.

I stepped back to the doorway of the kitchen and reached for the light switch that was beside it.

Thinking about it now, it was almost a metaphor, and like a flip of a switch, my life changed forever.

On the floor was a large rock placed right in front of the counter where my coffee pot was sitting. It looked like the rocks I had decorating my backyard. Behind the large rock was a path made from small smooth river stones.

Curiosity took ahold of me, and I followed them, flipping on light switches as I went, afraid of what would be in the next room. I followed the path through the hall where an overwhelming smell started to fill my nose.

I followed the stones into the dining room, which to my horror, was coated in red.

Every picture on the wall was soaked in it, covering it frame and all. The smell of wet paint was all you could breathe in. The table had a small centerpiece of red roses, dripped in red paint. Every placemat on the table was decorated with red splattered plates, bowls, cups, and napkins.

"Is this a joke by Robert?" I did not get it.

The stones continued through the dining room, into the foyer, and stopped at the front door. Taped to the door was an envelope.

I gently pulled it free and opened the envelope.

Inside were photos of my family, in our home, that were taken from outside the windows.

These looked like they were recent, I could not really tell. I was mainly going off how Brooke's hair was styled to place a time frame on it.

She was a 13-year-old girl after all and constantly went through different phases on how she styled her hair. She recently bought a hair crimper and had spent every night since crimping her perfectly straight blonde locks.

I was trying to wrap my head around what was going on. The rocks, the paint, the photos, nothing made sense. At that moment I could hear my phone's ringtone slicing through the silence.

I ran through the foyer and up the stairs. I could not bear going back through that eerie dining room setting.

By the time I reached my phone it had stopped ringing, but whoever it was left a voicemail.

I pressed the notification and listened.

The hair on my arms started to raise. Tears began to fill my eyes.

It was a recording of me screaming at Brooke to sit still and smile.

Hearing myself, it was too much. I was no mother, I was a director who barked out orders and beat her subjects into submission with condescending remarks and stabs to their self-confidence.

I sounded like a monster.

The worst part is that was not the first thought to come into my mind. Instead, I feared this being made public. Picturing people's reactions to my words. Words I spoke to my own daughter, it scared me.

DING DONG chimed through the house, causing me to jump.

Two more times it chimed. DING DONG. DING DONG. Followed by three loud knocks on the wooden door. After that, three pecks on the window.

I was frozen with fear.

Finally, I was able to move my hand to my side, and after that simple motion, I crumpled to the ground sobbing.

"What is happening?" I screamed.

My phone rang again. Unknown caller.

I could not bring myself to answer it, but I stood up, ready to hide if I so much heard any other noise from within or outside this house.

The screen abruptly turned blue. I dropped it to the bed. A picture started to come through; it was distorted but starting to come into focus.

No, it was not a picture, it was a video.

"Oh my god," I whispered, lips quivering, my body starting to shake.

There was my family. Robert, Ben, Brooke. All sitting by a pool in their bathing suits.

Not just any pool, but our pool!

Tears just started streaming down my face, blurring my vision, but I still could not escape trying to understand what I was looking at.

They were all sitting in a line against the wall of our elevated hot tub that slightly looked over the pool.

It was Brooke's favorite spot to draw. Legs dangling in the water, back propped up against the stone wall. Memories of Ben sneaking up behind her from the hot tub and ruining her work started to pour into my mind. I would never see that again. None of it.

They were forced to hold hands; you could tell by the thick black thread that was used to sew their hands together. Their lips stitched up to shape a huge smile. Painted with red on each their stomachs was a different word.

The three words formed a sentence, and it read:

"Thank You Mom."

I knew it was a video because the person holding the camera did not have a steady hand, giving away that this was not a photograph. Then he turned the camera to face himself after assuring I got a good view of my family.

It was the chauffeur. He looked deep into the camera, trying, and succeeding, to see directly into my soul. It could have been my mind playing tricks with me caused by shock, but I swear, there were tiny black wisps twirling in his pupils.

"I did you a favor," he said in a flat matter-of-fact tone. Then held up his hand. "You don't get to talk, I mean you can, and I can't stop you, but I can't hear you either. So, to make sure you do not miss out on what I am saying, I'd make sure you shut the hell up." He had a very posh accent. Really getting a close look at him, I could tell he was high maintenance.

He had such an intense look about him though, like he had purpose. His light brown curls just long enough to get caught in the blowing breeze. Finally, he blinked.

"Like I said, I did you a favor. You wanted to pretend you have this perfect life. Well honey, I am the only one who can give it to you. You see, your husband here... he was weeks away from leaving you. He did not even try to hide it. He already cleaned out his 401k, paid off your home... for you by the way. He really was a decent guy for someone who was leaving you for another woman." He pointed back at Robert, then to the kids lined up beside him.

"The kids knew. They have even gone on camping trips with him and his mistress. Now do not start to worry your little face. I have already deleted all trails of his affairs and his plans to leave you. It is just her word against the zero evidence she has if she ever brings it up. Now, your beautiful daughter over here... she was writing a novel, and you were the star! Her release date was just pending until after Daddy took her far away from you. That is right; she was jotting down all your secret flaws. Ben, well he was keeping you busy. He really knew how to play you like a fiddle." He leaned in close to the camera's lens.

"So, you have got two choices, Beth. I am going to call you again in a while. Answer and say, "Stop," and I will walk away. You can give the cops a shot at capturing your family's killer. OR answer and say, "Go," and I'll make this all appear like a tragic late-night accident." He paused again, allowing just enough time for all this to sink in.

He had this well planned out.

"All you'll have to do now is call the local police department. Give them a nice, concerned message regarding the trip your sweet little kids had won. Then go and clean up the dining room and the rocks. By the time you are done, the police should arrive with the heartbreaking news of your family's devastating end. Spending your time cleaning will allow you to look a little more distraught. I have a hard time believing you could pull away from your own selfish thoughts enough to look sad or worried. After that you can return to your perfect life!"

I started to think of what he was offering me. Is this a chance to start over? That thought was quickly shattered.

"But there is a catch to this, Beth. There is always a catch. If you say, "Go," you can never be anything but the perfect widow, the perfect mourning mother. You can never attempt to rebuild this life, even to try and better it or do it right. If you do, I will expose everything. Your past, your choice today, your daughter's book, your husband's plans to leave, and every detail of how it was done. It is all just a click away from being released to the world. We'll talk soon."

It could have been seconds or hours that I sat there, shaking, looking towards my bedroom window, knowing what horrible scene it would oversee.

I was still trying to process what was happening.

The phone rang. I answered, took a deep breath, and spoke.

"Go."

ABOUT THE AUTHOR

Paranormal Investigator

& Creator of Nightmares.
-Sounds cool until you find out about the

nightlight I have to sleep with.

Okay, you caught me; I'm weird.

I also refuse to write this in third person like I'm super dope
and not a hotmess who wears socks with sandals.

Check out my other work at GreathouseHorrors.com

Made in the USA
Middletown, DE
24 February 2023